PROFESSOR TOOTHY: THE FINAL LESSON

A Novelette By

JASON STEELE

For the teeth we've found along the way.

"Destiny is a worrying concept.
I don't want to be fated, I want to choose."
~ JEANETTE WINTERSON

CHAPTER ONE

The Professor

The sky above Grimstone University was gray and still. Cold drops of rain fell silently on the school's weathered stone walls as students made their way to class, unconcerned by the dreary weather. It always rained here, but rarely heavily enough to bother with umbrellas or raincoats. Instead, the students of Grimstone accepted a certain level of dampness as a fact of their collegiate life.

A short, stocky lion wearing a green argyle sweater vest stood upright on the far edge of campus, surveying an increasingly moist syllabus in her right paw. The lion's name was Talia, and today was her first day as a student at Grimstone. This was a school for those who lived in the Second Realm, a dimension full of magical beings who long ago fled Earth for fear of slaughter at the hands of humankind. Most of the students here had never even met a human, although they knew of their existence and knew it was unwise to seek them out.

Talia glanced around nervously—she had never seen so many people in one place before. The lion settlement she grew up in was quite small, and very far from any of the transportation hubs that connected the Second Realm. Her parents valued isolation, and she was the first of her family in more than a century to seek a life outside of their tiny community.

"Oh god," she thought to herself. "I don't even know what to call anyone." Her settlement had consisted only of lions, with the exception of an old eagle named Ziso who lived on the far edge of town. Ziso kept to herself mostly—which suited the lions just fine—but she had taken a liking to Talia, and was the one who had encouraged her educational ambitions.

Of course, there weren't just lions at Grimstone. As Talia's eyes darted from student to student she saw bug people, fish people, people made of bronze, people who seemed to be nothing more than floating garments, even people made of a thick blue vapor. It was a dazzling and diverse array of beings, and Talia had absolutely no idea how to respectfully address any of them.

"Need some help?" asked a friendly voice from up in the sky. Talia raised her head and saw a large, slightly patchy osprey in a dark denim jacket, gently flapping her muscular wings as she circled above. "You look like you're lost!"

"Oh!" said Talia, excited to see a bird person. She had spoken to a bird person before! "Yeah, I uh… this is my first day and I'm not sure where to go."

"The school is enchanted!" said the osprey, as she glided down and landed in the grass across from Talia. "It's called a guidance charm. Just walk around campus and you'll eventually end up at the class you need to be in. It's super disorientating at first, but you'll get used to it."

"Whoa, okay. Thanks." Her eyes fell upon the osprey's neck—there was an old scar there that extended all the way down to her chest. It looked extremely intimidating and cool, Talia thought.

"I'm Reah," said the osprey, folding back her wings and holding out one of her clawed hands. "Welcome to Grimstone!"

Talia extended her paw and grabbed Reah's hand, shaking it. "I'm Talia. I'm a lion!"

An amused look briefly flashed across Reah's face. "Yes, yes you are."

Talia felt her skin get slightly warmer, and she let go of Reah's hand. "Oh no, that was a weird thing to say. I've said something weird."

"A bit. You're from the outskirts then, right?"

"Yeah, way east of here. There's just lions there, and one eagle. I don't have a lot of experience talking with people who aren't lions."

"Just don't be a jerk, and listen to what people tell you, and you should be fine."

"Okay, I can do that!" said Talia, slightly louder than she meant to.

"Whose class do you have first?"

Talia looked down at her syllabus, which was now extremely damp and hard to hold straight. "Professor... Haste? For *Introduction to Spell Syntax.*"

"Ah. Dull class, dull teacher. Important stuff though, so try your best not to doze off. Trust me on that, I had to practically re-learn it all during my sophomore year and it was a huge pain."

"Thanks, I'll do my best."

Reah extended her wings and began flapping them, slowly lifting her huge body off the ground. "Well, I've gotta jet. I'll see you around, Talia the lion."

"Thanks for all the tips!" said Talia, awkwardly. "I'll see you around too, probably!"

Reah gave a friendly wink, and then soared off toward the center of the campus.

"She certainly has some muscles," thought Talia. "Oh hey, I talked to someone! I had a whole entire conversation! And I know how to get around now!"

She began walking toward the central campus, but quickly found herself compelled to veer right, away from the concrete path leading to the quad and instead toward an odd yellow stone building on the edge of the grounds.

"Oh," she thought, feeling disorientated just like Reah had said she would. "I guess my first class is over there."

The building was two stories tall and about as wide as four houses, constructed out of large irregular yellow stone slabs that all seemed slightly misplaced. The grass surrounding the structure was patchy and brown, and many of the windows on the second floor were shattered and sealed with black tarps.

As Talia approached, she noticed a black and silver plaque hanging next to the building's only door, which read: "PROFESSOR TOOTHY: DEPARTMENT OF TIME."

"Huh. I, uh, hope Reah wasn't messing with me," said Talia to herself, feeling like she would really rather not go inside. "No. Reah was super nice and she wouldn't do that to me. We're friends now. Lion and bird friends. Oh no, I don't even know what kind of bird she is!"

Talia felt slightly nauseous. She reached out her paw and grabbed onto the doorknob.

"It's okay that I don't know what kind of bird she is. She probably doesn't know what kind of lion I am." Talia paused for a moment, her eyes staring blankly at the doorknob. "Wait, what kind of lion *am I?* Wow. Hmm."

"Is someone there? You can come in, the door's open," shouted a high-pitched voice from inside the building.

"Okay! I'm coming in!" yelled Talia, and then she pulled open the door and stumbled inside.

It took a moment for her to understand what she was looking at. Hovering in the air near the center of the room was a figure who couldn't have been more than a foot tall, his pale body extremely smooth and oddly shaped. He had small four-fingered hands covered by soft white gloves, and long gangly arms that wobbled a bit as he moved. His face, which was almost the size of his whole body, was comprised of two large circular eyes, two thick black eyebrows, and a huge slanted mouth. He was a tooth. He was a living, floating tooth.

The tooth glided over to Talia, and gave her a little wave with his tiny right hand. "Hey!" he said, his treble voice thin and sharp. "I'm Professor Toothy!"

CHAPTER TWO

Strange Guidance

The inside of the yellow stone building resembled a warehouse, with its wide-open layout, industrial concrete flooring, and hanging fluorescent lights. Huge, archaic looking electronic devices were scattered around the room, beeping and buzzing and occasionally spitting out data on streams of perforated paper. In the very center of the building, hovering ominously above a large silver dais, was a sleek black pyramid about the size of a small car. The pyramid, Talia thought, gave off the unsettling impression that it was waiting for something.

"It looks like it might just be you this year," said Professor Toothy, floating over to a particularly noisy machine. "Some years I actually end up with *no* students. I'm afraid *Time Studies* isn't a very popular class these days. There's just not a lot of work in the field. The sad truth is, no one has made any significant progress in decades."

Talia looked down at her syllabus. She was definitely in the wrong class.

"Look, I'm not trying to discourage you from being here, but I want to make sure you understand what you're getting into," said Professor Toothy. He whacked the side of the noisy machine and it became even noisier. "The only reason this class even still exists is because the dean has a special interest in the subject. Otherwise, I'd be completely out of funding."

"I think… I'm in the wrong class," said Talia, staring intensely at her syllabus and avoiding eye contact with the professor. "I'm so sorry, it says here I should be in *Introduction to Spell Syntax* with Professor Haste right now."

"Oh!" Professor Toothy's body seemed to deflate slightly. "Of course!" He floated over to Talia and took at look at her syllabus. "Yes, that is a much more reasonable class for you to be taking, especially in your first year!"

Talia shifted uncomfortably. It was her first day of college and already she had disappointed someone.

"Tell me," said Professor Toothy, with a contemplative look on his face. "Why did you walk all the way to this lab? It is quite a bit out of the way."

Talia wasn't sure how to answer, so she decided to just tell the truth, even if it made her sound absurd. "This cool bird woman told me that the school magically guides you to your classes, so I just walked where I felt like it was directing me."

Professor Toothy handed Talia back her syllabus and then slowly floated away, stroking his head.

"Did I get pranked? Is this some sort of hazing?" asked Talia.

The professor turned and looked at her with an expression of intense seriousness. "The school's guidance charm leads you to wherever it is you need to be. Generally, it will lead you to class. In cases of emergency, you will feel compelled to leave the school entirely. In this particular instance, I have absolutely no idea why you were led here. But there must be a reason, and likely an important one."

Talia suddenly felt very prickly and warm. This was all sounding far too ominous for her first day. "So, what should I do, professor?"

"I can show you the way to Professor Haste's class, guidance charm be damned, and you can take the class you were expecting to take." Professor Toothy floated toward Talia, looking even more serious than before. "Or, just for today, you can stay here and see if my course interests you. Perhaps you're meant to do great things in the field of time! If you find that this sort of research calls to you, I'll get you scheduled here officially."

Talia looked around the room, her eyes studying the strange equipment and artifacts. She wasn't sure how she would know if any of it was calling to her.

"Of course, it's not impossible that the school's guidance charm made a mistake. If you don't like what you see here I will write you a note for Professor Haste, and you can continue with him tomorrow."

"This is all very weird, but I'll give it a shot," said Talia, mostly out of a desire to not further disappoint the professor. "I just have one question."

"Of course, what would you like to know?"

Talia looked at the floating black pyramid in the center

of the room, and pointed her paw at it. "Is the pyramid alive?"

Professor Toothy's face fell completely flat, and he seemed to almost lose his balance, dropping a few inches from the height at which he was hovering. "Why would you ask that?" he said, his voice slightly unsteady.

"Oh god, have I said something wrong?"

"No! Not at all, no. But please, why would you ask me that?" The professor was somehow looking even paler than his usual extremely pale self.

Talia hesitated for a moment. She wasn't sure why her question had evoked such an intense response, and didn't want to further upset him. "It just feels like it's alive, doesn't it? Like it's waiting for something? Watching us and stuff? I dunno, I guess that's a creepy thing for me to think about a pyramid."

"No. Well yes, it is a very creepy thing to think. But you might not be wrong."

Talia swayed a bit. Now she was feeling anxious about having possibly disrespected the pyramid in some way.

"That pyramid is one of the few objects in the world that we know has traveled through time. You see, the material it's made out of is actually much older than the universe itself. So, at some point it was sent backward in time, and possibly more than once. It's been at the center of our time research here at Grimstone for more than two hundred years."

Professor Toothy turned to the pyramid and held out his hand, as if to feel for something invisible in the space between him and the hovering dark object. Talia wondered if she should be trying to feel something as well.

"Those who have studied the pyramid long enough begin to feel what you feel—that the pyramid is alive somehow, that it's waiting. Watching us. To be honest, it's very spooky and none of us have at all enjoyed the experience."

"I feel very spooked and I've only been here a few minutes," said Talia, who was indeed feeling quite unnerved.

"Well, that's exactly why I'm so surprised. It took me fifteen years of near-daily contact before those odd feelings began to creep into my mind," said Professor Toothy, looking back to Talia. "You've only just arrived and already you can feel the life force of the pyramid."

"Oh. Huh. I don't like that."

"I don't like it either. For one, I'm a little jealous that you have an immediate connection with the ancient floating pyramid I've dedicated my entire life to researching. But, also, this has me fully wigging out about the pyramid again, which is something I haven't done in a long time."

Professor Toothy floated over to an office chair and plopped down into it.

"You get used to being around a huge floating pyramid that might be alive, and that might be watching you," said the professor. "It becomes a regular part of your day. But now, because of all this, it's back to feeling irregular. Very irregular and freaky."

Talia felt herself swaying again. "I didn't mean to make things freaky, I'm sorry."

Professor Toothy shot up from his chair. "No! You have nothing to apologize for, this is the first promising thing to happen with my research in years! It's just, you know, my research happens to involve the terrifying unknown. These things happen!"

The professor sped over to a small cabinet in the far back of the room, then returned holding a loaf of bread and some water.

"Homemade ciabatta! You look like you might pass out, eat!"

"Thank you," said Talia, taking the bread and water and then sitting down on the floor.

"I'm sorry, I would offer you meat but I'm a vegetarian," said Professor Toothy.

"Oh, this is fine!" said Talia, biting into the ciabatta. "I like bread."

The ciabatta was delicious. It had a pleasant flavor with a lacy, porous texture and a crispy yet chewy crust. Professor Toothy was a excellent baker.

Soon Talia was feeling up to standing again, and the professor showed her around the building, explaining the specific functions of the various beeping machines. All the while she could feel the black pyramid's strange, otherworldly gaze following her every move. And as more and more time passed she could feel something else, too. Whatever the pyramid was waiting for, whatever it had waited nearly all of time to see, it was going to happen soon.

CHAPTER THREE

Ghosts

Directly to the west of Grimstone University sat a tall, modern looking building that served as the school's dormitories. A sign at the top of the structure read "Student Housing & Third Gateway," in bold red letters. Given that there were no discernible gateways on any floor, the words came across as eerie and sinister, and it was a regular source of amused discussion amongst students.

Talia's dorm was on the seventh floor, which was much higher up than she was comfortable living. She didn't have a fear of heights per se, but she definitely felt more at ease when she knew her paws were on solid ground.

The events of the day were feeling less like things that had actually happened, and more like weird, distant dreams. Exhausted, Talia stumbled into her dorm room's shared living area and collapsed onto a couch near the door. It was one of the room's only pieces of furniture, and she loved dramatically throwing herself on it.

"How was your first day?" asked Ula, a six and a half foot tall woman made entirely out of dark indigo crystals. Ula was Talia's roommate, a fellow freshman at Grimstone who was studying to become a professional necromancer.

"The school's guidance charm sent me to the wrong class, but it turns out I was meant to be there because an ancient pyramid wanted to watch me or something."

"I see," said Ula. Her voice was deep and multi-layered, as if it were echoing against itself and splitting into beautiful harmonic tones. "I am glad to hear you had an interesting experience."

"Yes, it was definitely interesting." Talia rolled off the couch and onto the floor, her face pressing against the gross carpet. "I have to decide whether I want to keep going to the creepy pyramid class or just go to the class I'm supposed to be taking."

Ula walked forward, carefully stepping over some books that Talia had dropped on her way in. Ula's footsteps were unnaturally silent, as if she weighed nothing at all.

"How was *your* day?" asked Talia. She turned her head to look at Ula, but from her current position all she could see were her legs.

"Uneventful. Uninteresting, even. I have been a practicing necromancer since I was a child, but it is illegal without a license, so I have to pretend I don't already know all of the things they are going to teach me this year."

"That sucks," said Talia. The texture of Ula's crystal body, Talia noticed, was not stationary. It looked like there was a faint fog slowly swirling inside her.

"I am not a master yet, so eventually this school will have things to teach me. Until then, however…"

Talia sat up, and rested against the couch. "Wait, so you can do necromancer stuff? What sort of stuff?"

Ula kneeled down next to Talia, and held out both of her pointy crystal hands. "Touch my palms, I will show you."

"Okay sure, why not."

Talia pressed her paws against Ula's palms. Ula closed her eyes, and quietly mouthed some sort of incantation. The fog inside her crystals started swirling more quickly, as if a storm was forming. Suddenly, hundreds of small ghostly bugs began shooting out of Talia's body.

"Whaaaaaat, no no no no!" yelled Talia, bolting up and stumbling back onto the couch. It took only a few moments for there to be ghost bugs everywhere—crawling up the walls, buzzing through the air, slithering across the floor—it was like something out of a nightmare.

Ula waved her hands and mouthed another word, and the bugs vanished.

Talia sat on the couch breathing heavily, holding her paws tightly against her face. "That was really rad but please don't do it again."

"Most of necromancy is ghoulish and alarming, which is likely why you need a license to practice it," said Ula, standing herself up again.

"What was it you just did, exactly?" Talia's breathing was still very rapid, and for the tenth time today she felt herself getting lightheaded.

"I summoned the ghosts of every bug you have ever killed."

"Wow, that makes it even more terrifying."

Ula looked down at her hands. "I have a confession,

Talia. When we met yesterday, and we shook hands, I performed a similar spell."

"Oh?"

"Yes. I summoned the ghosts of every person you had ever killed, and of course none appeared. It is a thing I do."

Talia realized she still had her paws on her face, and moved them to her side. "That is… wow. Have you ever caught a murderer?"

"Yes," said Ula, her layered voice sounding even deeper than before.

"Oh my god, who?"

"My mother."

Talia's paws shot back up to her face. "No way! That sucks! I can't believe you're telling me this!"

"It was… a difficult day, when I found out."

"Who did she kill? You know what, I'm sorry, I shouldn't be asking this."

"Dozens of souls poured out of her. My mother had murdered a truly monstrous number of people."

"Oh my god oh my god oh my god…" Talia began involuntarily rocking back and forth. "Why? Why did she kill so many people?"

"She told me that our family had long ago learned how to gain strength through the infliction of suffering and death, but that we abandoned the practice due to changing times. She told me that she was simply reclaiming our ancestral right as beings of immense power."

Ula glanced over at Talia, who was looking extremely disturbed.

"I apologize," said Ula, "I have made it a personal goal to be more open with people here, and I think it was perhaps too soon to share such a thing. I did not mean to upset you."

"Are… you alright? When did this happen?"

"Two years ago. It was the catalyst for my decision to come to Grimstone, and acquire the credentials needed to practice my craft within the rule of law."

"Yeah, I can see how that would have a big impact on the direction of your life."

There was silence for a few moments, as both Ula and Talia tried to think of more to say.

"I think I might make some dinner," said Ula, turning and walking toward their shared kitchen. "I believe I know enough about lion physiology to put together something we can both eat."

"Sure, uh, let me know if you'd like some help."

Talia laid herself down on the couch and stared up at the ceiling. There was an odd stain that looked like someone had thrown a slice of pizza up there. In the kitchen, Ula began collecting ingredients from their small refrigerator and placing them on the counter.

"Ula," said Talia, unsure if she wanted to continue her thought.

"Yes Talia?"

"If someone did that spell on you, would any ghosts come flying out?"

Ula began filling a large pot with water. After the pot was about halfway full, she turned off the water and said, "Only one."

CHAPTER FOUR

A Terrible Warning

Talia stood outside the door of the yellow stone building, shivering slightly as the chilly morning rain slowly soaked both her fur and her red sweater vest. She had been standing there for fifteen minutes, unable to go inside. She hated disappointing people more than almost anything in the world, and today she was going to disappoint Professor Toothy.

"The wetter I get the more anxious I'm going to feel doing this," said Talia to herself. "Also I'm late now. I got here slightly early and now I'm late."

Talia gave a great big lion sigh, and then sat down on the ground and leaned against the door. Why was this so difficult? Why was it so hard to advocate for herself, to make a decision based on what *she* wanted instead of what *others* wanted?

"Sorry about that!" yelled Professor Toothy, floating across the grass toward the building.

Talia looked up in surprise. "Oh! Hello!" she replied, clumsily getting to her feet.

"It's quite embarrassing, I've dedicated my life to the study of time and yet I so easily seem to lose track of it! Let me unlock the door…"

The professor waved his hand and a large brass key materialized, which he pushed into the lock.

"There we go. I'm so sorry you were stuck out here in the rain!"

"Actually I, uh… don't worry about it," said Talia, following the professor into the building.

After only a few steps she could feel it—the presence of the black pyramid. The sensation was stronger today, clearer. It knew she was there, and had been expecting her.

"Would you like any tea?" asked Professor Toothy as he circled the room, turning on the various machines.

"No thank you," said Talia, wondering how long she should wait before breaking the bad news.

Soon the sounds of beeps and hums had filled the room, and Professor Toothy was hovering over his desk, gathering some papers.

"Professor…" said Talia, her paws fidgeting nervously.

"It's okay that you don't want to take the class, Talia," said Professor Toothy, turning toward her. "If your heart's not in it, this field of study will be torture. It's mostly torture even if your heart *is* in it."

"I really wanted to like it!" said Talia, apologetically. "And I know the guidance charm really wants me to be here…"

"I firmly support fighting against whatever destiny the

universe tries to inflict upon you. It's your life! You need to forge your own path!"

"Thank you for being so…" started Talia, but before she could complete her sentence there was a terrible blast of purple light that knocked her to the floor, and sent Professor Toothy crashing onto his desk.

A strange black fog seeped in the room, quickly rolling along the floor and filling every corner and crevice. It shuttered for a moment, and then instantly vanished, leaving behind the intense stench of burning plastic.

Talia got to her feet, shaken and dazed. "Professor, what…" started Talia, but again she was interrupted, this time by an unbelievable sight. Floating in front of her, wearing some sort of unusual metallic helmet, was a second, older Toothy.

"Hey Talia!" said the older Toothy, waving to her. "I'm Doctor Toothy!"

"Doctor?" asked Talia, holding one of her paws to a bruise that was beginning to form on her head.

"Oh, I haven't been a professor in many years. Speaking of which…" Doctor Toothy turned to Professor Toothy, who had gotten up from his desk and was staring wide-eyed at his older self. "We need to talk, professor!"

"Yes, I imagine we do!" said Professor Toothy, his voice unsteady.

"I am you, from the future, as I'm sure you've deduced. Yes, you discover the secrets of time travel, but I can't explain how or else terrible things will happen."

Talia decided she would feel better being on the ground again, and sat herself down.

"This is incredible, I haven't wasted my life after all!"

said Professor Toothy, tears welling up in his eyes. "So many years have gone by with no results, but now this…"

The professor reached out his hand to touch his older self, but it simply passed through the doctor's body as if it were a ghost.

"This is a projection, professor. I cannot travel here physically, only as reflected light. Please, there isn't much time… I only have enough power to do this for a few minutes a day."

"Of course! What is it you've come to tell me?" asked Professor Toothy, shaking with excitement.

"The humans. They discover our realm and destroy it. So many of our people are murdered, so many good people…" Doctor Toothy stopped talking and stared off into nothing, seemingly caught up in the memories of the terrible future he now lived in.

"How could that happen?" asked Professor Toothy, his voice now steady. "They do not possess the magic necessary to cross over into this dimension!"

"There is a man who discovers a way in," said Doctor Toothy, snapping back into the moment. "And he brings other humans with him, thus beginning a long and brutal campaign of death that leaves our world desolate and empty."

Talia decided that sitting was not enough, and laid herself down flat on her back, nauseated and confused. Her second day of college was going even worse than the first.

"What can I do?" asked Professor Toothy, his eyes focused and intense.

"The man responsible for the destruction of our world,

our people, his name is Stan Bolinski. You must travel to the human realm and find him."

The professor's face was suddenly looking very grim and uncertain.

"Yes, of course. But, I don't know if I can kill someone. I don't know if I have that in me."

"You don't need to kill him," said Doctor Toothy. "There is a much less violent solution."

Talia tried to sit up again, but she was feeling way too dizzy and laid herself right back down.

"What do I need to do?" asked the professor.

"A year from now he will accidentally stumble upon information regarding the nature of interdimensional travel during an extraordinary kitchen mishap. He cooks himself a lamb chop dinner, and things just sort of go super wild."

Talia looked up from the floor, trying to figure out if she heard what Doctor Toothy had said correctly.

"What sort of kitchen mishap could possibly lead to information like that?" asked Professor Toothy.

"The specifics are unimportant. What's important is, I believe this entire terrible future can be avoided if he simply never cooks that dinner. If on that fateful night instead of cooking himself a large batch of lamb chops, he does literally anything else."

"Yes, yes I understand," said Professor Toothy, pacing back and forth in the air. "I just need to figure out a way to ensure he never cooks those lamb chops."

"I have had much more time to think about this than you, and I believe I've developed the optimal strategy. You must travel to Stan in the human realm, and force-feed him lamb chops every day until he develops a permanent negative association with the meat. I know we're vegetarian and this is going to be super uncomfortable, but it's far more ethical than any of the alternatives."

"Yes… yes that could work," said Professor Toothy, pacing faster now. "I'll make him so sick of lamb chops that there's no way he'll willingly cook them himself."

The form of Doctor Toothy slowly began to distort, and the strange black fog re-appeared. Talia bolted up from the ground and stumbled around unsteadily as the fog slithered around her legs.

"I can stay here no longer, but I will return if I am able! Please, you must find Stan and stop this nightmare before it begins! I know you can do it, because I myself could absolutely do it! Good luck!"

There was a loud bang and a purple flash of light, and Doctor Toothy was gone. Talia slumped down onto the floor again, and Professor Toothy collapsed into his office chair. For a few moments they were both completely silent.

"I will find him tonight." said Professor Toothy, his voice strong and determined. "I will find him and I will shove lamb chops down his throat, to save our world."

"I definitely do not want to take this class," said Talia. "This class is very upsetting and I don't think I can deal with it."

"I understand. Thank you, Talia, for giving it a shot."

"Good luck with the lamb chop thing."

Talia slowly stood herself up and gave Professor Toothy an awkward salute, then shuffled out the door. The rain, she noticed, had gotten even colder.

CHAPTER FIVE

The Duck

As the sun started to set over Grimstone University an unpleasant breeze developed, making the already brisk rain feel downright chilly. The enchanted floating lanterns lining the grounds flickered themselves on, rocking unsteadily in the wind. It was around this time of day that the campus usually quieted down, but tonight, somewhere in the distance, far enough not to be seen, an extremely loud duck was angrily screaming.

The scream was easy to hear through the poorly insulated walls of the campus dorms, and many of the students were sticking their heads out of their windows, wondering what the duck could possibly be going on about. It sounded as if the duck was having an absolutely volcanic tantrum, and wanted everyone at the school to know how upset they were.

"That is an impressively loud duck," said Ula, sitting on the couch and reading a large spell tomb.

"Do you think they're in trouble?" asked Talia, her head completely out the window.

"No," said Ula, flipping forward a few pages in her book. "I have heard the screams of trouble, of pain. These are whiny screams, screams of temper."

"Oh," said Talia. "I'll take your word for it."

Suddenly a huge bird flew up to Talia and hovered, flapping, in front of her. It was Reah, the osprey she had talked to the previous morning. Talia jumped in surprise and hit her head on the window frame.

"Hey, Talia right?" said Reah.

"Yeah," said Talia, trying to regain her composure. "You're Reah! You're a bird!"

"Yes, yes I am a bird," said Reah, both amused and annoyed. "Please don't call me a bird again, just my name is fine."

"Oh, yeah, of course. Sorry." Talia felt like sliding out of the window, down the wall, and burying herself in the ground.

"You wanna go check out that screaming duck?" asked Reah.

"Sure, why not! I'll go see a duck."

"Great! Does your roommate want to come?"

Talia looked over to Ula.

"Her roommate appreciates the offer but would rather stay as far away from the screaming duck as possible," said Ula, continuing to flip through her book.

"Cool, just you and me then," said Reah, and she grabbed Talia with her mighty legs and pulled her out of the window.

"Oh my god!" yelled Talia, very surprised to suddenly be seven stories in the air with nothing to stand on.

"You alright?" asked Reah, as she flew toward the sounds of the screaming duck. "My talons didn't get you, did they?"

"You're good!" lied Talia, who had indeed been pierced by Reah's talons but found, surprisingly, that she kind of liked it. Reah's legs were strong, and muscular, and very much in control, and Talia enjoyed the sensation of being gripped so intensely.

"I'm pretty sure the duck is behind the library, which is right over there."

Reah increased her speed, effortlessly carrying Talia through the air toward Grimstone's large, ancient library.

"I haven't been to the library yet," said Talia. "Is it a good one?"

"It's spooky," said Reah, "but yeah, lots of super old books. Hard to find what you're looking for though—I think someone put a curse on the place a while back or something, because the layout is constantly changing. Even the librarian has a hard time keeping up with things."

"Oh. That sounds obnoxious."

"I think that's the duck," said Reah, as they passed over the library.

Sure enough, stomping around in the grass behind the library was a very large, screaming duck. Not a duck *person*, of which there were many in the Second Realm, but just a regular looking, abnormally large duck.

"Oh god, they're as big as a bathtub," said Talia.

"Let's see what they're screaming about," said Reah, but

Talia could not hear her. The duck's screams were now so loud that they drowned out all other sounds.

Reah dropped Talia onto the grass, and then floated down beside her. They both began to cautiously approch the duck, who quickly noticed them and immediately ceased screaming.

"Hello," said the duck, in a deep, calm voice that projected a sense of authority and competence. "My name is Mr. Craw. As you have no doubt surmised, I am a giant duck. Much larger than the ducks you are likely used to seeing."

"Yeah, we know you're a duck," said Reah, who continued approaching Mr. Craw. "Why were you screaming your head off?"

"Ah," said Mr. Craw, turning slightly so that he was facing Talia instead of Reah. "I believe I was screaming for you."

Talia blinked. "For me? Why were you screaming for me? I don't even know you!"

"This is incredibly embarrassing, but I actually have no idea," said Mr. Craw.

"How could you have no idea?" asked Reah, whose posture had become quite aggressive. "What are you playing at, duck?"

"It's Mr. Craw," said Mr. Craw. "I was once a regular duck, but I swallowed a magical amulet and both my size and intelligence inflated. And my ego, if I am to be honest, so I would appreciate it if you would call me by my name rather than my species."

Reah's stance loosened a little. "Right. Sorry. Why don't

you explain why you were screaming for my friend here, Mr. Craw."

"Yes, of course," said Mr. Craw. "I was in the middle of migrating, as I am known to do, when I felt an extraordinary magical pull toward this university. I recognized it at once as a guidance charm, which is present at many large institutions and not at all unusual. What I found odd, of course, was that it was attempting to guide *me*, and I neither go to this school nor have any business here."

Talia sat herself down in the grass. She felt like this was somehow going to be about the pyramid, and it was making her grumpy.

"I followed the guidance, curious as to why it was happening, and it led me here. Then it instilled in me an intense desire to scream as loudly as I possibly could. Finally, the moment I saw you," said Mr. Craw, turning again to Talia, "all of those compulsions went away. I feel none of them now. I have no idea what the purpose of any of this was, or why the guidance charm felt like this was the easiest way to bring you here, but that is what happened, and that is why I was screaming."

Mr. Craw ruffled his feathers a bit, and then stretched out his wings and took off into the air.

"Farewell! I hope my screaming was not a terrible bother to anyone!"

Talia collapsed backward onto the grass and groaned. Reah, watching Mr. Craw disappear into the distance, sat down next to her.

"Well, that wasn't really what I was expecting," said Reah.

"The charm brought Mr. Craw here because I wasn't listening to it," said Talia, sighing.

"Wasn't listening to what?"

"It's been trying to get me to leave my dorm ever since I got home. I ignored it, because I think it wants me to do some sort of creepy time travel stuff."

"Uh… okay, you're going to need to elaborate on that."

Talia told Reah all about her unusual couple of days, and how she didn't feel mentally equipped to deal with any of it. As she talked, the sun fully set and the area behind the library became very dark, lit only by two magical lanterns on either side of the building.

"I can see why you're overwhelmed," said Reah. "That is *very* different than my first couple of days here were. The weirdest thing that happened to me was my bed turning into a bunch of snakes. Which was pretty weird, but not like what you've been going through."

"Snakes?"

"There's a lot of snake-based prank magic. A lot."

"Oh no," said Talia, quickly sitting herself up.

"What's wrong?" asked Reah, but she knew the answer before she had even finished speaking.

A huge squirrel was approaching them from the wooded area behind the library. Again, as with Mr. Craw, this was not a squirrel person, but a regular squirrel, only much larger. The squirrel had a solid black dagger in her mouth, which she spit out onto the ground in front of Talia.

"Uh, there," said the squirrel. "That's for you, I think. I don't know why, but it's for you. I was digging for it all day. Again, I don't know why."

The squirrel turned and began heading back into the woods.

"Don't tell anyone about me!" yelled the squirrel. "I don't like people!"

"Okay!" yelled Talia.

Reah picked up the dagger and examined it. The blade, the handle, all of it was made out of a peculiar, smooth, extremely black material which was not unlike whatever the pyramid was made out of.

"That's a pretty nice dagger to get stabbed with," thought Talia, and then she wondered why in the world she had thought that.

"Dude, your destiny is rad," said Reah, holding the dagger out for Talia.

"Keep it, I don't want my destiny or that dagger," said Talia, grumpily.

"You want me to carry you home?" asked Reah.

"… yes."

Reah scooped up Talia with her sturdy bird legs, and lifted her into the sky.

"I like being carried around," thought Talia. "I want to be carried everywhere."

As they ascended higher and higher, the lanterns below began to look like fireflies fluttering in the wind.

"Beautiful."

CHAPTER SIX

It's Not Going Well

To Talia's great relief, nothing particularly strange happened during her classes the day following the duck incident. *Introduction to Spell Syntax* had been exactly as dull as Reah had warned, but the mundane, steady pace of Professor Haste's teaching was exactly what her anxious mind needed right now.

She had also attended her first *Magical Sequencing* class, which she found utterly compelling from start to finish. Her teacher, Professor Luca, was a slender gray cat woman who was extremely passionate about the subject. The purpose of the class was to demonstrate the various ways in which spells could change depending on the order of the words used to cast them. Talia had a natural talent for connecting ideas and figuring out how stuff worked, so this sort of thing was completely up her alley. Toward the end of the lesson she began to wonder what it would take to break into the field of spell writing.

As Talia made her way back to the dorms to turn in for the night, she noticed the lights were still on in Professor Toothy's lab. Should she check up on him? It would certainly be a nice thing to do, but what if something creepy happened again? The day had been so pleasant, why should she risk ruining it by voluntarily throwing herself back into that absurd situation? Then again, she wasn't feeling any strange compulsions to go, which meant the guidance charm didn't think there was anything important there that she needed to see. So, she reasoned, nothing too bizarre could happen if she went, could it?

"I'm going to go," thought Talia. "I'm going to go and it's not going to be weird. I'll see how he's doing and then head home and eat some snacks and pass out."

A few minutes later Talia had arrived at the yellow stone building, and she let herself in through the unlocked door.

"Professor Toothy?" said Talia, looking around the room. It was much messier than it had been yesterday—sheets of data were unevenly taped to every wall, the various beeping machines had been haphazardly pushed together on one side of the room, and all over the floor there were puddles of a sticky, purple goo.

"Ah! Talia! I wasn't expecting to see you!" said Professor Toothy, floating up from behind one of the machines. He looked like he hadn't slept since yesterday. "I'm glad you stopped by, I've been getting a little too far into my own head today. It'll be good to talk to someone who isn't me, or someone I'm force-feeding lamb chops to."

"How is that going? The lamb chop thing?"

"It's not going well, honestly." Professor Toothy floated over to a counter and took out a tea pot. "Tea?"

"Sure, why not," said Talia, who had never actually had tea before.

"Is oolong okay?"

"I don't know what that is, but sure."

"Most of my favorite teas are oolong. I think you'll enjoy this."

The professor began steeping a pot of tea, and Talia walked aimlessly around the room, making sure to step over the strange purple goo puddles.

"What's not going well?" asked Talia. "If you don't mind talking about it."

"I found the man that my future self described. It was a trivial matter, to be honest, humans are very easy to track. I teleported to the human realm last night, and then again this afternoon. Both times I successfully forced the man to consume lamb chops, and he is beginning to show signs of disliking them. I'm going to visit him again tonight, right before he goes to sleep. Perhaps he will have lamb chop nightmares."

"That sounds like everything is going according to plan. According to your weird, weird plan," said Talia, narrowly missing a goo puddle. "So what's wrong?"

"It just... it feels like I'm missing something important. The man just doesn't seem like the sort of person who would initiate a genocidal campaign against our people. He's a boring guy with a boring job. What if what I'm doing now is what turns him bad? What if me force-feeding him lamb chops gives him the motivation to find and destroy us?"

"Time stuff continues to sound like a nightmare," said

Talia. "I have a hard enough time making decisions when I have a reasonable idea what the outcome will be."

The tea was finished steeping, and the professor poured it into two cups.

"Here," said Professor Toothy, floating over to Talia. "It should be the perfect drinking temperature. These are enchanted cups."

"Oh cool," said Talia, taking a sip. She had no idea if it was indeed the *perfect* temperature, but it tasted good.

"Sorry about the goo," said Professor Toothy, floating over to the array of beeping machines. "Now that I know my research eventually succeeds, I've been accelerating my work. Most of it has yielded… disappointing results."

"Like the goo?"

"Yes, I accidentally opened a portal to the goo dimension for a few seconds today."

"The goo dimension?" Talia continued sipping her tea.

"A whole dimension filled with nothing but goo. You'll actually learn all about it if you're taking *Interdimensional Travel* this year. It's believed there used to be intelligent life there, but they messed something up real bad and now there's only goo."

Talia looked down at one of the goo puddles. "Is the goo dangerous?"

"No, at least not anymore. It's just goo now. Who knows what it used to be."

Professor Toothy ripped a print-out from one of the beeping machines and began to study it.

"Has your future self visited again?" asked Talia.

Professor Toothy looked up from the print-out, with a worried expression on his face.

"No. And I'm not surprised. My future self has, potentially, dramatically changed the course of both history and our own life. It's possible I will never actually figure out time travel magic now. Or maybe I do figure it out, but this lamb chop thing was successful and our world was never invaded, so why would I risk messing the timeline up just to say hello?"

"I hadn't considered all the paradox stuff. That sounds really heavy."

"It is extremely heavy. I can't sleep. It's making my work sloppy. I can't be sloppy right now, so much is on the line."

"Well, I believe in you professor. I don't know you all that well, but, uh, you just seem like the sort of person who is going to succeed. You're gonna do it. It's gonna get done, because of you. Professor Toothy, Time Commander."

Professor Toothy gave a faint grin. "You know, in all my years of time research no one has ever called me Time Commander."

"That's probably a good thing. Calling you Time Commander is basically just calling you a huge nerd."

"Well, I am a time wizard at a magic school who hides away in his laboratory with his computers."

"Those are computers?" said Talia, looking over at the beeping machines.

"Technically, yes. Just very, very old, from the days in which people were actually making computers for time research."

"Yeah I guess you are a huge nerd. Time Commander it is, then."

Talia had finished her tea, and she set the empty cup down on the counter next to the pot.

"I should probably head home, professor."

"Thank you for stopping by. I hope the tea was to your satisfaction."

"Yes, it was quite satisfactory, thank you," said Talia, and she gave a little bow. "Good luck with the lamb chops, and saving the world."

The professor sighed. "Or destroying it. The night is young."

As she lay in bed that night trying to sleep, Talia could feel the charm pulling her again, but much more gently than it had before. The dagger, she needed to get the dagger. Not now, but soon. Very soon she would need to possess the black dagger, and use it to stop something terrible.

CHAPTER SEVEN

Forty Seven Portraits

The room was an iridescent pearly white, every inch of which was smooth and polished and flawless. Sleek, sparkling walls stretched upward and upward, disappearing into the foggy infinite above. On each wall hung various silver portrait frames, forty seven in total, only a quarter of which actually contained portraits. The people in these portraits looked solemn and melancholy—a snake woman staring into the middle distance, a metal man with crossed, rusting arms, an old tree person with brown withering leaves, and so on.

In the center of the room there were silver trinkets floating waist high in a grid-like formation, as if they were pieces on display at a celestial museum. And in the center of the trinkets sat a round cushioned sitting area, upholstered with a thick, dark gray fabric.

Talia could not recall how she had arrived in this room, and she wasn't entirely sure it was even real. It felt imagined, incorporeal, even though she could see it and touch it. Time seemed to move differently here, like it was stretching itself out and then clumping itself back together. It wasn't unpleasant, being in this room, it was just sort of fuzzy, like she was trying to grasp at something but it kept slipping through her paws.

"You're in a dream," said a familiar voice, deep and harmonic. Talia turned and saw Ula, relaxing on the edge of the sitting area and examining one of the silver trinkets. "It's just not *your* dream."

"Oh. Hey Ula. So is this... *your* dream?" asked Talia, cautiously walking toward the trinkets.

"Yes. I apologize, I should have told you about this possibility sooner. I, like many in my family, have psychic dreams that can sometimes drag in other unconscious people. It is uncommon, but I find that lately it has been happening more often."

"Oh god, I wouldn't want someone else seeing *my* dreams. Would you like me to try and wake up?"

Ula shook her head, and then stood up. She was even taller in her dream than in real life, and absolutely towered over Talia.

"Have you seen the portraits?" asked Ula, as she walked toward one of the walls. "They are incomplete, but one day I hope to fill each frame."

"Who are they?" asked Talia.

"These are the forty seven people my mother killed in her quest for power."

"Ah. Yeah." Talia wasn't sure what to say. She wasn't used to people sharing dark, personal things with her, and although she wanted to be supportive it all made her a little uncomfortable. "Why are most of them empty?"

"In order to absorb her victim's power, my mother had to collect their souls. I have taken it upon myself to track down the families and friends of each of the people she killed, and return the stolen souls to them. Every time I return a soul, I put the person's portrait up on one of my dream walls."

Talia looked around at the portraits, and then back at Ula. "It seems like," said Talia, "you're carrying around a lot of guilt that isn't yours."

"I know that I am not responsible for her cruel acts. I know that it is not my burden to right her wrongs." Ula's voice became deeper, almost guttural. "My mother was, for most of my life, my hero. I modeled so much of myself after what I saw in her, and she encouraged it. She hollowed me out and filled me with herself, and I was overjoyed to have it done."

Talia put her paw on Ula's back, and said, "But you *aren't* like her. Even with all the influence she had on you, you still ultimately made very different choices."

"That is why I have given myself this responsibility. Who we are is how we act, what we do. The only way I can prove to myself that I am not her, that I am not driven solely by selfish impulses, is by trying to soothe the wounds she left on this world."

"Well, that's a lot to put on yourself, but you do what you need to do to feel alright."

Ula walked over to a row of floating silver trinkets.

"Why is it you have avoided the tasks the guidance

charm has attempted to recruit you for, even though you know of their potential importance?" asked Ula.

"It's complicated," said Talia, who walked over to the sitting area and dramatically flopped herself down directly in the center of it.

"We do not need to speak of it if you do not want to. It may have been rude of me to ask such a question."

"No, it's fine, I'm just easily overwhelmed," said Talia. She rolled around on the cushions for a moment and then looked back over at Ula. "It would be different if I knew what the plan was, or why the guidance charm was trying to manipulate me into doing stuff. But as it stands I have no idea what's actually going on, and for all I know the charm is trying to get me to do something terrible."

"I see," said Ula, putting down a trinket. She walked back to the sitting area and sat down next to Talia.

"Think about it," said Talia. "The guidance charm has, so far, given me a black dagger and led me to a hovering black pyramid. If I end up unwittingly opening up a portal to a hell dimension, do you know what people will say? They'll say, 'Well, obviously something like that was going to happen. Everything the charm had her do was so super evil sounding, how could she not have seen that coming?' And I would be like yeah, you got me there. I really shouldn't have plunged the death dagger into the angel box, that was a rookie mistake for sure."

"Yes, you have a point," said Ula. "I had not considered the possibility that the charm's intentions could be malicious. Malicious intent is apparently a blind spot of mine."

"I will absolutely show up for an important fight if I

know who I'm fighting and why, no matter how anxious it makes me. But I just can't deal with the ambiguity. I don't want to be the person who ruins everything without even meaning to."

Ula laid herself down next to Talia, and they both stared up into the foggy infinite for a while. The room seemed to slowly swell and contract, as if it were breathing, and Talia found the effect to be extremely relaxing and meditative.

"How long do these room-dreams of yours usually last?" asked Talia.

"Only a few hours, but in here it can feel like days. I'll sever our psychic link so you can get some actual sleep."

"Ah, yeah, thanks."

"I have appreciated our chats. Thank you for listening, and for sharing."

"Uh, no problem."

"Sleep well," said Ula. She waved her hand and Talia floated up into the fog.

CHAPTER EIGHT

Last Call

The endless rain at Grimstone University was unusually heavy today, pelting the campus with thick cold pellets which were pooling up unpleasantly in the muddy grass. Talia was thankful that she didn't have any classes scheduled, and decided to lounge on the couch and do some *Magical Sequencing* course work, which was far and away her favorite subject.

At around noon there was a noise at the door, followed by what sounded like a deep, harmonic curse word, and then another noise as the door swung open and Ula walked in, soaking wet.

"My wet crystal hands were having a hard time turning the knob," said Ula, dripping onto the carpet.

"Wow, uh, let me get you a towel," said Talia, setting down her textbook.

"Thank you."

Talia grabbed the largest towel she had—a novelty she

had purchased at a transportation hub during her voyage to Grimstone. The design printed on the front was of an extremely toned dragon woman at the beach, flexing suggestively.

"Here," she said, handing the towel to Ula. "It's the biggest one I have."

"This is some towel," said Ula.

"That it is."

As Ula dried herself off, Talia went into the kitchen to reheat some leftovers.

"I'm going to eat, do you want anything?" asked Talia, taking a covered bowl out of the fridge.

"No thanks, I only eat once a day," said Ula.

"Oh, I did not know that. Noted."

An intense feeling suddenly took hold of Talia. It was like the pulling sensation she felt when the guidance charm was trying to bring her somewhere, but instead of feeling like a suggestion it felt like an urgent scream.

"Oh no," said Talia, carefully putting the bowl back into the fridge with her shaking paws.

"What's wrong?" asked Ula, who had just finished drying herself.

"I'm feeling the guidance charm again, but it's different this time. It's more urgent, and resisting it feels kind of painful."

Talia slumped to the floor and put her paws on her head.

"Stop it. *Stop.* I'm not going to listen to you, charm, get out of my head."

The sensation immediately stopped.

"Oh. Uh, that worked. It just went away."

Ula walked over to Talia and kneeled down beside her. "What was it trying to get you to do?" asked Ula.

"It wanted me to visit Professor Toothy's lab, right away. But I don't want to. Am I being irresponsible? Is it okay if I don't go?"

"Talia, it's always okay to make your own choices. However… hmm, may I offer you some advice?"

"Sure," said Talia. "I'm pretty freaked out right now and advice would be good."

"You don't know the motivations of the charm that has been leading you around, and you're worried that it's trying to trick you into making a terrible choice. It very well might be. But if that's the case, it will likely call upon another student if you fail to comply. And that student might not have your instinct to question what's being asked of you. You can follow this through to the endgame, and choose to not perform whatever final task it has for you. Yes, you are likely putting yourself at personal risk by going, but the risk doesn't seem to be the part of this that's holding you back. Unless I've misread the situation."

"No, you've read it pretty well, and you make some good points," said Talia, as she stood herself up. "Alright, well, while I'm feeling this momentary sense that it's actually an okay idea to go, I'm going run over to Toothy's."

"Would you like me to accompany you?"

"No. I mean yes, but no, it should probably just be me. I don't know why, but that's the feeling I have."

"Good luck, Talia."

"Thanks!" said Talia, as she hurried toward the door. "If I die and the school ships my stuff back to my parents, don't let them send the towel!"

CHAPTER NINE

No More Lamb Chops

The door to the yellow stone building swung open, and an absolutely drenched Talia rushed inside. The rain had become downright torrential, and a strong, cruel wind lashed droplets around like shrapnel against anyone unfortunate enough to be outside.

"Talia! Goodness, what are you doing out in this weather?" asked Professor Toothy, floating over.

"I'm not sure. The guidance charm wanted me to come," said Talia, who was very out of breath.

"Oh, how peculiar. I was actually just about to make my next trip to the human realm. Perhaps that's why it called you?"

"Yeah, maybe. I don't feel anything from the charm now though."

"Why don't you sit over there by the machines," said Professor Toothy, pointing to the beeping equipment that was still bunched up on one side of the room. "They emit a lot of heat, it should warm you up and help dry you off."

"Okay, thanks," said Talia, who shuffled over to the machines and collapsed in front of them.

"I'll just be a few minutes. When I come back, the world will be a couple of lamb chops closer to being saved!"

"Sure. Good luck, professor," said Talia, who was feeling exhausted.

There was a brief flash of light, and then Professor Toothy spiraled around in the air, emitting a colorful cloud of sparks. Less than a second later he was gone, magically transported away to the human realm.

Talia sleepily leaned against one of the machines. It was indeed very warm, and it felt nice against her soggy fur. She shut her eyes and listened to the hums and beeps of the equipment. It was calming, like being in a strange mechanical forest.

"Hide."

Talia heard this word inside her head, with her own voice. She opened her eyes and immediately tensed up. Why did she think that? Why did that word show up in her mind? She looked around the room—there was no one there but herself. She was alone.

"Hide."

It was louder this time, more desperate. She got to her feet and looked out the nearest window. All she could see was rain.

"HIDE."

Her mind was practically yelling it now. Shaking, she ran to a spot behind the machines and hid, completely out of sight from the rest of the room.

There was another burst of colorful sparks, and something spiraled into the room and thumped against the floor. Talia peaked through a small gap between the machines to get a glimpse of what had happened, and then gasped. It was Professor Toothy, lying on his side, gurgling and sobbing.

"His enamel…" thought Talia, horrified. "What happened to his enamel?"

The surface of Professor Toothy's body and face had been burned away, exposing a fleshy muscular structure underneath that was itself slowly deteriorating. He looked like he was moments away from death.

Talia began to stand up, to rush over and help, but the voice in her head returned even louder than before.

"NO!" it screamed. "Not yet!"

Talia kneeled back down, frightened and confused. Was this the moment she needed to disobey? Why would the charm bring her here if it didn't want her to help?

There was a blast of purple light. A familiar black fog rolled into the room, shuttered, and then vanished. Doctor Toothy had arrived.

"Oh my, what happened?" asked Doctor Toothy, floating down to the dying professor.

"He… sugared me. A whole bag," said Professor Toothy, slowly sputtering out the words as his body withered away. "I… don't know if I did enough. To stop him. I just don't know…"

"You did enough," said Doctor Toothy, in an eerily joyous tone.

Professor Toothy looked at him for a few seconds, and then said, "Your body, your face… why isn't it burned?"

"Hmm, good question, Professor!" said Doctor Toothy, menacingly.

The form of Doctor Toothy shimmered for a moment and then faded away, revealing a new form, the form of an old hawk man.

"… Simon?" said Professor Toothy, in disbelief.

"It should be *Professor* Simon, but you convinced the educational board to revoke my license, didn't you?"

"That was ten years ago… you were out of control," said Professor Toothy, his voice sounding coarse and weak.

"Thirty years ago for me. You see, I continued my time research in private, and it worked! I figured it out, Toothy! And do you know what your future self is up to? You're trying to take it all away from me, *again!* You've made it a government concern, and any day now they're going to steal my research and lock me away. Why? Because *Professor Toothy* can't stand the idea that *Simon* succeeded where he failed. Because you can't stand the thought of me having a little *power* for once! Because you want that power only for *yourself!*"

"There needs to be… strict oversight… with any time magic," said Professor Toothy, gasping. "It's so dangerous… so unbelievably… dangerous…"

"Just so you know, before you die," said Simon, crouching down next to the professor, "killing you was incredibly boring. This is almost the hundredth time we've done this little routine, and thank *god* I finally managed to pick a human who sugared you. I wish I could've done it myself. Maybe one day I'll perfect the magic and do just that. I have so much more time now with you out of the picture! Ha, ha ha! Farewell, professor."

With a loud bang and a purple flash of light, Simon was gone.

Talia rushed out from behind the machines and ran over to the professor, whose breathing had become very slow and strained.

"Professor!" yelled Talia. "I'll go get the medical staff! Oh god, oh god…"

"Talia," said Professor Toothy, his voice now only a whisper. "You have to stop him… with time… any other way, and he'll know… he'll get you too…"

"I don't know how to do time stuff, I don't even know where to begin!"

The professor's breathing slowed even further, and then stopped entirely. His body went limp. His face was frozen in an expression of pain and sorrow. Professor Toothy was dead.

CHAPTER TEN

The Lion, the Dagger, and the Pyramid

The rain outside the yellow stone building began to thin, and the howling wind quieted down. Talia sat, stunned, next to the lifeless deformed corpse of Professor Toothy. She had never seen someone die before, and this had been a particularly horrific death to witness. She thought that she should be crying, but no tears came. She was too drained, too empty. Nothing felt real.

"What do I do?" thought Talia. She suddenly realized that she was still staring at the professor's body, and jerked her head away. "Oh god, what do I do?"

What had been the purpose of the guidance charm leading her here, or anywhere? As far as she could tell her presence had neither helped nor harmed anything. How did it all connect?

"Magical Sequencing," she thought to herself. "I like figuring out how things fit together, and why. I can apply that to this."

The black pyramid, the black dagger—the charm had led her to both. How were they connected? They both seemed to be made out of similar substances. What did they do, what was their purpose?

A spark of realization formed in her head. What if she wasn't considering the whole picture, what if the charm had been responsible for things she hadn't even noticed?

"Ula," thought Talia. "What if Ula being my roommate wasn't by chance? What if…"

The pieces began to fall into place, and Talia was pretty sure she knew what it was she needed to do.

* * *

"Excuse me?" said Reah, in an alarmed tone.

"I brought you here because I need you to stab me in the heart with the dagger," said Talia.

Reah and Ula were standing in front of the black pyramid, staring at Talia with worried expressions.

"Ula, it's possible to capture a person's soul in a vessel, correct?" asked Talia.

"Yes. I have seen it done, as you know."

"I think the floating pyramid is a sort of time machine, and this dagger is my way in."

Ula and Reah looked at the pyramid, which was silently hovering above its silver dais.

"How did you come to this conclusion?" asked Ula, in a way that suggested she was choosing her words very carefully.

"I've been able to feel a presence inside the pyramid ever since I first entered this room. Professor Toothy told me that every researcher who has ever worked here eventually started feeling like the pyramid watching them, like it was alive. For me, that feeling has been getting clearer and less abstract every day. And now, I understand why. The pyramid *is* alive, because I'm already inside it."

"You're... already inside it?" asked Reah.

"It's spooky time stuff, I don't understand how it works I just know that it *did* work, because I'm already in there."

Ula began examining the pyramid. She gently rested her hands on one side of it, then looked over at Talia. "I feel something. It is very faint though. I would say it is possible you are not incorrect."

"Alright, so let's say you're in the pyramid," said Reah. "How do you know you need to get stabbed by the dagger to get in?"

"The guidance charm led me to the pyramid and the dagger. They're both made out of the same stuff. I also just so happened to become roommates with someone who has experience with soul transference rituals. I'm not, like, 100% sure about all this, but the pieces do connect!"

"Let me see the dagger," said Ula, and Reah reluctantly walked up and handed it to her. "Hmm, well there is certainly some sort of magic in this dagger, but it's nothing I've encountered before. If it does indeed capture souls, I'm not certain I have the knowledge to be able to perform a transference between it and the pyramid."

"The guidance charm thinks you can do it, and that's good enough for me," said Talia.

"Why do you want me to be the one to stab you?" asked Reah. "I don't give off a... stabby vibe, do I?"

"There's no way I can do it myself. And you're

extremely, uh, physically fit, and I have a feeling the dagger needs to go all the way in to work."

"Gross. But thank you, I am indeed super buff," said Reah, mock flexing.

"Please, I need to do this before I lose my nerve. If I think about it too much longer I might freak out and run off," said Talia.

"That would not be an unreasonable course of action," said Ula, and she handed the dagger back to Reah. "However, if this is the path you wish to take, I will assist you."

"I'm not going to risk letting the world be ruined by a guy who has that much power over *all of time*. I have to do this," said Talia.

"Alright, I'm in. I really hope you're right," said Reah, "because if you're not I'm definitely going to jail for this. And also you'll be dead, which would be a huge bummer."

Talia stepped in front of Reah. "Make it quick, if possible. I'm sorry if I get blood all over your jacket."

"If you do it'll be a way cooler jacket," said Reah, and she gave a worried smile. "Are you sure it needs to be your heart?"

"No. But that's what feels right and I don't have much else to…"

Before Talia could finish, Reah drove the black dagger directly through her chest and into her heart, plunging it all the way to the hilt in one smooth blow.

"Gah," said Talia, faintly. There was pain, but only a little bit, and also a fluttering of excitement. "Thanks for surprising me. That… that was definitely the way to go."

"No problem, buddy," said Reah.

There was a loud, deeply melodic cracking sound, and Talia's body disappeared into the dagger. Reah gasped and jumped back, dropping the dagger onto the ground.

"Oh no! I'm sorry Talia, I dropped you!" she said, carefully picking it back up.

"That... I have never seen before," said Ula. "When souls are taken, the bodies generally do not go with them."

"Here, take it, I've done my bit," said Reah, handing the dagger over to Ula. "Oh wow, I did get blood all over my jacket. Weird, this is so weird."

Ula walked over to the black pyramid and touched the dagger to it. "I know a few soul transference spells, I'm going to start with the simplest one."

She began humming in slow, harmonic tones, and immediately the dagger absorbed itself into the pyramid and disappeared.

"Oh," said Ula, frowning. "It's usually a much longer process. And usually the vessel doesn't merge with the receptacle. I really have no idea what sort of magic is at play here."

"Well, we did it!" said Reah, throwing her hands in the air. "It's all up to Talia now!"

* * *

Talia was used to seeing time as a progression from one point to another. It was linear, it moved in a single direction, and you could watch as it played out in front of you. That was no longer the case for her, and she couldn't tell how long it had been like this. How long had she been in the pyramid? Did she just get here, or had she always been? She could see every moment of the pyramid's existence, all at once, and it was somehow not overwhelming.

Her friends, Ula and Reah, were waiting in the lab for her to come back. Meanwhile, Professor Toothy was dying on the floor, and he was also entering the lab for the first time as a student. A million years in the future the pyramid was buried, hidden, not to be dug up again for yet another million. A billion years in the past it was splitting off from a larger object, an object the pyramid would only ever see again once.

It was hard to think in here, because everything was already thought, the decisions were already made, she had already left, already returned to her friends. Where was the moment, the moment she had come here for?

There it was. Simon had collected the pyramid and brought it somewhere else, somewhere secret. With Professor Toothy dead he was free to use it in his own research. He was walking toward it, so close, within inches. The pyramid extended a piece of itself out, piercing his skull. Simon was dead, and now his body was decaying, gone, and now it was done.

* * *

The rain outside had returned to its usual inconsequential drizzle, and there were even tiny rays of light peaking through the gray clouds, something that rarely happened in the skies above Grimstone. Inside the yellow stone building Ula was carefully examining the black pyramid, as Reah sat against a wall in the back of the room.

"How long do you think we should wait?" asked Reah.

"I could not begin to guess," said Ula, and she walked away from the pyramid.

"I've never stabbed anyone before," said Reah. "I mean, I slashed someone with a knife once in a fight, but like, neither of us were really trying to kill each other."

Ula sat down next to Reah, and said, "Committing an act of violence, no matter the purpose, can have a profound effect on one's mind."

"Do you think I should like, talk to a professional about it? Is that what you're saying?"

"I think we should both probably talk to a professional after this. Talia, too."

There was another loud, melodic cracking sound, and Talia's body began to ooze out of the pyramid, reforming itself on the silver dais below.

"Talia!" yelled Reah, running over to the dais with Ula. "You're alright! Oh, god, *are* you alright? Are you still stabbed?"

Talia looked around the room, dazed. She felt like she had been gone for an impossibly long amount of time.

"Please tell me you're not still stabbed!" said Reah.

Talia was beginning to understand words again, and put her paw against her chest. "No, I don't think I'm still stabbed," said Talia, and Reah gave her a big hug.

"It is so good that you're not still stabbed," said Reah.

Ula and Reah helped Talia up, and walked her away from the pyramid.

"Oh, no," said Talia, noticing the remains of Professor Toothy. "He's still dead."

"What happened in the pyramid?" asked Ula.

"I'm still trying to parse it all in my brain. I was

everywhere in time, maybe? I could see, like, billions of years of stuff all at once. I'm... oh god, I'm still in the pyramid," said Talia, and she collapsed to the ground.

"You're not in the pyramid, it's okay," said Reah as she sat down next to Talia.

"No, I mean I'm always going to be in there now. It's... giving me a headache thinking about it."

"We don't need to talk about this now, we can discuss it when you've rested," said Ula.

"No!" said Talia, aggressively. "Sorry, no. I feel like I'm already starting to forget stuff, like when you wake up from a dream. I need to say it all now."

"Well, the important things then. Were you able to find Simon?" asked Ula.

"Yes, I stabbed him in the head," said Talia.

"Whoa," said Reah. "That means we're stab buddies now. Have *you* ever stabbed anyone, Ula?"

"Yes," said Ula, but she did not elaborate.

"Cool. Stab Club, that's us now," said Reah. "I'm going to make a Stab Club stencil and paint it on jackets for us."

"I must have killed him after he had already killed the professor, or something," said Talia. "I can't believe Toothy's still dead."

"You wanna, uh, go back in and try again?" asked Reah, darkly.

"I can't. The pyramid kept the dagger," said Talia.

"You did well," said Ula. "This was a huge risk you took, and it worked."

"Thanks," said Talia. "I think... I actually need to pass out now."

And with that, everything went black.

CHAPTER ELEVEN

The Infinite

Talia opened her eyes, but everything looked blurry, formless. She heard what sounded like beeping in the distance, and humming, lots of humming. The room was bright, but she couldn't tell how bright. A dark shape appeared in front of her.

"You're awake," said a deep, harmonic voice.

"Ula?" asked Talia, and she tried to sit up, but didn't have the strength.

"You're in the campus medical center. You've been out for a few days," said Ula.

"Oh. Am I okay?"

"I think so. Your doctor didn't seem particularly worried."

"Cool." Talia closed her eyes again and fell back asleep.

A few hours later there was a clanking sound, and Talia awoke with a jerk.

"Sorry, sorry!" said Ula. "I tripped over a chair."

Talia could see where she was now. It was a small, sterile looking medical room with a bed and a few chairs, as well as an odd, vaguely mystical looking cylindrical device next to the door that was slowly spinning and humming.

"It's okay," said Talia. "How long have you been here? Don't you have class?"

"Our classes for the next week have been postponed, because of the investigation," said Ula.

"Investigation?" asked Talia.

"Well, a teacher was killed on campus and a student was attacked, and they don't know how it happened."

"A student was attacked?"

"That would be you," said Ula. "Reah and I reasoned that if we explained what actually occurred it might create a paradox, and Simon might avoid his death."

"Ah. Well, I can't think that strategically right now, but I trust your judgement."

"Speaking of Reah," said Ula, "she dropped this off earlier today."

Ula handed Talia a tweed jacket. On the back in bright green stenciled paint were the words "STAB CLUB," along with a demon skull and two crossed daggers.

"It's perfect," said Talia, and she hugged it.

"I got one too, but I'm not particularly fond of my stabbing memory," said Ula. "I'll have to talk to her about that before this *Stab Club* thing gets out of hand. I think she's just excited that you're not dead."

"I'm pretty excited about that too," said Talia, remembering the moment when Reah had plunged the dagger into her chest. Was it strange that she thought the experience of getting stabbed by Reah had been intense and beautiful? Scary and painful, yes, but it had been such a perfect stabbing—vigorous yet precise, balletic almost.

"What are you thinking about?" asked Ula, having noticed that Talia was zoning out.

"Oh, uh, nothing," said Talia, embarrassed. "Okay, I was thinking about how me getting stabbed was kind of beautiful in a weird way."

"I… suppose?" said Ula, who did not sound like she had found the sight of Talia getting stabbed in the heart at all beautiful.

"When I was in the pyramid," said Talia, feeling awkward and wanting to change the subject, "I saw the beginning of it. The moment the pyramid formed. It had belonged to a much larger object, and it was splintered off and sent on its own, eventually ending up on our world."

"That is an extraordinary bit of knowledge," said Ula. "Do you have any idea as to its purpose? Was it sent here for a reason?"

"I don't know," said Talia. "The farthest I could see back was the moment it split from the bigger piece. I remember floating away, as the larger form watched. It was huge and lumpy, and made out of the same material."

"Maybe it was lonely," said Ula. "You were there, watching it, because of its extraordinary time properties. Perhaps this is its way of meeting people?"

"Ula, you are super deep and I'm glad you're my friend."

"I aim to impress."

"I hope I was okay company. I mostly remember just being kind of confused for billions of years at once."

"Do you recall anything from the future?" asked Ula.

"Oh, wow, let me think about that for a second. Most of the pyramid's future is spent buried underground. I have many, many memories of just dirt and stuff."

"Was there some sort of disaster?"

"No, I think it just kind of got tossed away at some point by people who had no idea what it was."

"How anti-climactic."

Talia dug deep into her memories from her time in the pyramid. It was hard to sort out the order of things, as everything appeared to happen at the same moment while she was in there.

"Eventually it was dug up, I remember that," said Talia. "Dug up and brought somewhere. It was... oh!"

Talia shot up in bed. "It was brought back to the thing it had come out of! The big object made out of the same stuff! It wasn't as big at that point, I guess it had sent a bunch of itself away."

"Extraordinary," said Ula. "Who brought it back there? How did they figure out where it had come from?"

"I can't remember," said Talia. "It's bizarre, I can remember it being dug up, being carried, loaded onto some sort of ship, but I can't..."

Talia's face went pale, and she fell back into bed.

"Talia? What's wrong?" asked Ula, moving her chair closer.

"There wasn't anyone else there, it was just me," said Talia.

"So it was moving on its own?"

"No," said Talia, turning to face Ula. "*I* was moving it. *I* was there, me. Physical me, looking just like I do now, but millions of years in the future."

Ula leaned in and put her right hand on Talia's forehead, then mouthed a few words in an old language. As she did this, her crystal hand began to glow bright white and emit an intense heat, at which point she stopped muttering and drew her hand away.

"I'm sorry," said Ula, in an extremely deep and sympathetic tone.

"What's wrong?" asked Talia, but she had a pretty good idea what was wrong.

"This is only a guess, please understand that."

"What's wrong with me, Ula?"

"It is possible that when the pyramid reconstructed your body, it did so using its own material. If that is so, you may now be functionally immortal."

Talia extended the claws in her right hand, and plunged them into her left arm. When she removed them, the wound healed instantly.

"Oh my god," said Talia, astonished.

"I don't know what to say," said Ula, solemnly. "A life without death… it's unthinkable to me." She put her hand on Talia's shoulder. "I will do everything in my power to help you on this journey, Talia."

Talia lay there, stunned, staring at the ceiling. Then, slowly, she put her paw over her chest.

"Well, on the bright side," thought Talia, her face forming an impish smile, "this means I can ask Reah to stab me again."

Printed in Great Britain
by Amazon